The Three Bears
Holiday Rhyme Book

Written by Jane Yolen
Illustrated by Jane Dyer

SCHOLASTIC INC.
New York   Toronto   London   Auckland   Sydney

To Brooke and Cecily, who were there
from the beginning of Baby Bear
—J. Y. and J. D.

ISBN 0-590-97548-X

Text copyright © 1995 by Jane Yolen.
Illustrations copyright © 1995 by Jane Dyer.
All rights reserved. Published by Scholastic Inc., 555 Broadway, New York, NY
10012, by arrangement with Harcourt Brace & Company.

12 11 10 9 8 7 6 5 4 3 2 1   6 7 8 9/9 0 1/0

Printed in the U.S.A.   14

First Scholastic printing, September 1996

The illustrations in this book were done in Winsor and Newton watercolors
    and Rotring artist's colors on 140-lb. Waterford hot-press watercolor paper.
The display and text type were set in Adroit Light by
    Harcourt Brace & Company Photocomposition Center, San Diego, California.

Contents

New Year's Eve

They never let me
Stay up late
To help the big bears
Celebrate,
But make me go
To bed at eight.

So on my bed
I toot my horn
To welcome in
The New Year's morn
And baby New Year,
Freshly born.

That means that I
Can always be
An hour early
(Maybe three)
To celebrate
Most noisily.

Lucky me!

Groundhog Day

Around the corner, down the road,
and right next door to Mr. Toad,
lives Mr. Groundhog in a home
made of mud and dirt and loam.

Now Goldie says he's very shy,
a quite retiring sort of guy.
He never stays up very late;
he never goes out on a date.

In fact, except for once a year,
nobody even knows he's here.
But come that day, and Mr. G.
goes right outside to see if he

can see his shadow on the ground.
First he looks up, then he looks down,
and if he spies it, goes back home,
back to that house of dirt and loam.

Of course, if he no shadow spies,
it isn't thought a great surprise.
He *still* just shrugs and goes right home,
back to that house of dirt and loam.

No shadow means an early spring;
a shadow seen—the other thing:
a longer winter, lots more snow,
and icy winds that chill and blow.

I cannot think that it's much fun
to live away from sky and sun
and only come out once a year,
but Goldie says that's why he's here.

His job's to do the best he can,
for he's the woodland Weather Man.

Valentine's Day

I always tell my Mama Bear
That I love her a lot.
I always give my Papa Bear
The biggest hug I've got.
And Goldie is my closest friend.
I'm sure she knows it well.
So who I sent a valentine
Is something I won't tell. . . .
But his initials are B. B.
So, maybe you can guess—
It's me!

St. Patrick's Day

I'm Irish
Yet I'm bear clear through.
How can that be?
I wonder, too.
But Goldie says
On St. Pat's day
We're green and Irish
All the way.
So hip-hurrah
In my bright green hat,
A happy holiday,
St. Pat!

Earth Day

I am the Earth
And the Earth is me.
Each blade of grass,
Each honey tree,
Each bit of mud,
And stick and stone
Is blood and muscle,
Skin and bone.

And just as I
Need every bit
Of me to make
My body fit,
So Earth needs
Grass and stone and tree
And things that grow here
Naturally.

That's why we
Celebrate this day.
That's why across
The world we say:
As long as life,
As dear, as free,
I am the Earth
And the Earth is me.

I AM THE EARTH

AND THE EARTH IS ME.

Arbor Day

Do bears love trees?
They love them lots,
When birds lay eggs
Up in the tops.

Do bears love trees?
They love them very—
Apple trees and pear
And cherry.

And bears love trees
When bees are home,
The hollows filled
With honeycomb.

Do bears love trees?
Oh, sure bears do.
Since I'm a bear,
I love them, too.

May Day

Goldie's basket
Glows with reds.
Roses nod
Their velvet heads.
Tulips tip
With every breeze,
Trying very
Hard to please.

In my basket
Gold and green
Are the colors
To be seen.
Black-eyed Susans,
Daffodils,
Dandelions
From the hills.

Which is nicer
For the day?
Which is really
Right for May?
Goldie says that
Both are fine.
But don't you think
That you like mine?

Mother's Day

Who was it cradled me
Soft in her tummy?
Who was it fed me
On milk and sweet honey?
Who was it rocked me
To sleep every night?
Who was it showed me
The wrong from the right?
You were, dear Mama,
You taught me to say
I love you, I love you.
(Especially today.)

Father's Day

Not another necktie,
Not a pair of socks,
Not some red suspenders
In a great big box,
Not another handkerchief,
Not a pocket comb,
Not another store-bought card
With some silly poem.
Close your eyes and think real hard.
Bet you won't guess this:
HERE'S A GREAT BIG BEAR HUG
AND A SLOPPY KISS!

(Oh—and if you think that's all,
Don't be really sad.
Here's a pair of bedroom slippers
For my favorite dad.)

INDEPE

Independence Day

Rockets write
Across the sky
INDEPENDENCE
Ten feet high.

Firecrackers
In the air,
Signaling
To Baby Bear.

Up above,
Let freedom ring;
Down below,
The bears all sing,

Caroling
A nation's song—
Ten feet high,
A lifetime long.

Labor Day

Mama Bear works
and brings home money.
Papa Bear works
and brings home honey.
So once a year
we celebrate
how hard they work
by sleeping late.

Halloween

When Goldie and I
Go trick-or-treat
At every house
On Forest Street

Our bags get full,
Our feet get sore,
But still we want
Just one treat more.

So why—when we
Have just come home
To share our cake
And honeycomb—

Are we too pooped
To eat at all?
We leave our bags
Out in the hall,

And fall asleep
Without a bite.
It happens *every*
Halloween night.

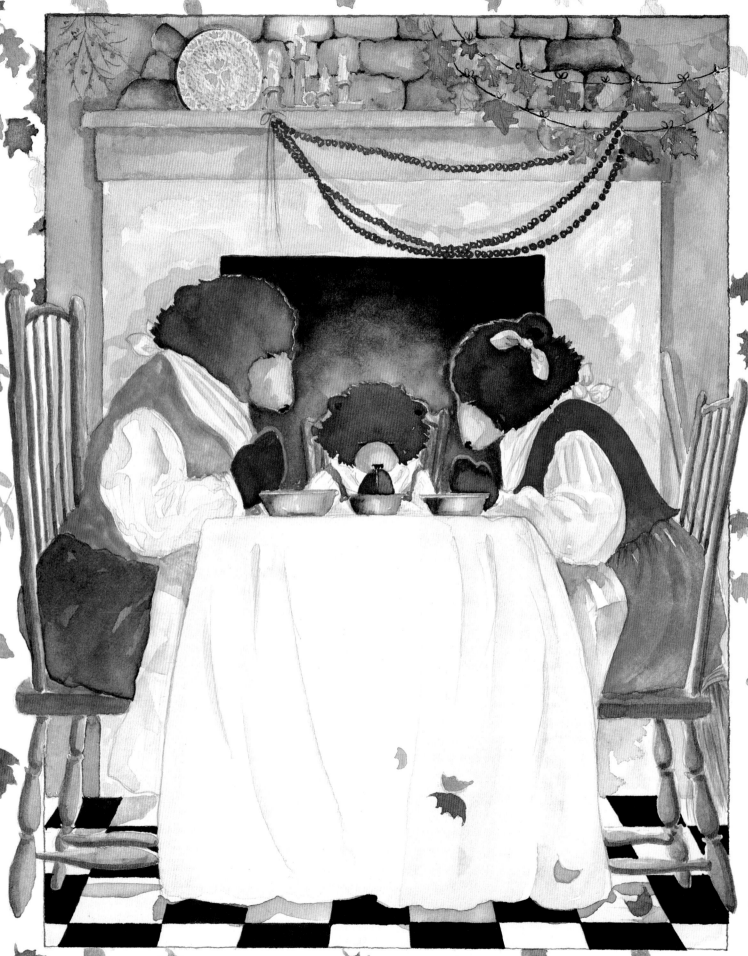

Thanksgiving

Thanks for forests,
Thanks for trees,
Special thanks
For honeybees.

Thanks for porridge,
Thanks for chairs—
Thanks for all
My special bears

Thanks for Goldie,
Once again,
Thanks from Baby Bear.
Amen.

Christmas & Chanukah

Stars are shining
Down the lane,
Making halos
On each pane.

Celebrations
For a night
Made of holy
Candlelight.

For each candle
Say a prayer.
Blessings on us,
Every bear.

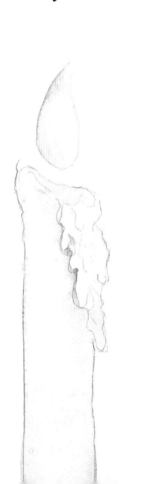

Happy Birthday

Here's the cake,
Candles lit.
Take a breath;
Think a bit.

Make a wish;
Blow with care.
Happy Birthday,
Baby Bear!